friendly phonics

A Talking Telescope

By Cindy Leaney

Illustrated by Sue King and Peter Wilks

ROURKE CLASSROOM RESOURCES
The path to student success

Note to Parents and Teachers/Educators

Before reading: Ask your child what this book might be about. Read the title aloud together. Then ask what sound the letter *t* makes in *talking* and *telescope*. The name *Thomas* has a *t* sound even though *th* often makes other sounds. Remind your child to listen for the *t* sound in the story.

Written by Cindy Leaney
Designed by Ruth Shane
Illustrated by Sue King & Peter Wilks
Project managed by Gemma Cooper

Created and Designed by SGA and Media Management
18 High Street, Hadleigh, Suffolk, IP7 5AP, U.K.

© 2004 Rourke Classroom Resources
P. O. Box 3328, Vero Beach
Florida, 32964, U.S.A.
Editor: Patty Whitehouse.

Printed in China

ISBN   1-58952-918-9

A Talking Telescope

Thomas has a telescope to look
up at the stars.
He likes to look at planets like
Jupiter and Mars.

Tonight it is terrific. There are too many stars to count.

I'll take you to that tower that I told you all about.

Let's go to the tower and climb
right to the top.

We can take my telescope and
try to set it up.

Oh, that's absolutely perfect. You got here just in time!

I see Thomas has his telescope but you might like to try mine.

Who said that? Who's that talking?
Quick, turn the flashlight on.

There's nothing but that telescope.
The person must have gone.

It was me, the telescope. Yes, point
the light just here.

I've been waiting for someone to turn up–
for years and years and years.

I've got lots of things to tell you.

One or two tricks to teach you, too.

Some tips for looking at the stars,

the planets, and the moon.

Now take a look at Jupiter.
Try counting Saturn's rings.

They are terrific aren't they?
Truly beautiful things.

We're lucky that we met you. We've seen fantastic sights.

The sky is like a treasure chest that opens every night.

Game time!

Can you unscramble these words from the story?

1. tgo

2. ghtin

3. copteeels

4. emt

5. ytr

6. kaet

Fill in the missing letter *t*s to find new words. What are they?

1. _ oy

2. _ ime

3. _ op

4. _ able

5. _ urtle

6. _ rip